DINOSAUR GHOST

by Erin Soderberg
Illustrated by Duendes del Sur

ABDOPUBLISHING.COM

Reinforced library bound edition published in 2017 by Spotlight, a division of ABDO. PO Box 398166, Minneapolis, Minnesota 55439. Spotlight produces high-quality reinforced library bound editions for schools and libraries. Published by agreement with Warner Bros. Entertainment Inc.

Printed in the United States of America, North Mankato, Minnesota.
042016   092016

THIS BOOK CONTAINS
RECYCLED MATERIALS

PUBLISHER'S CATALOGING IN PUBLICATION DATA

Names: Soderberg, Erin, author. | Duendes del Sur, illustrator.
Title: Scooby-Doo and the dinosaur ghost / by Erin Soderberg ; illustrated by Duendes del Sur.
Description: Minneapolis, MN : Spotlight, [2017] | Series: Scooby-Doo early reading adventures
Summary: Scooby and the gang are digging for dinosaur bones for the museum when some of the bones go missing. Did a dinosaur ghost take them? It's up to the gang to find the missing bones and save the exhibit.
Identifiers: LCCN 2016930645 | ISBN 9781614794646 (lib. bdg.)
Subjects: LCSH: Scooby-Doo (Fictitious character)--Juvenile fiction. | Dogs--Juvenile fiction. | Dinosaurs--Juvenile fiction. | Ghosts--Juvenile fiction. | Museums--Juvenile fiction. | Mystery and detective stories--Juvenile fiction. | Adventure and adventurers--Juvenile fiction.
Classification: DDC [Fic]--dc23
LC record available at http://lccn.loc.gov/2016930645

Spotlight
A Division of ABDO
abdopublishing.com

Scooby and the gang were helping Velma's Uncle Ted dig up dinosaur bones.

The bones were going to be used for a dinosaur exhibit at the museum.

"Like, this is hard work," Shaggy said. "I'm ready for a snack."

"Reah," added Scooby.

Uncle Ted wanted to show
Velma and her friends the
bones that had already
been found.
But when he opened the box,
he saw something he did
not expect.
"Oh no!" Uncle Ted cried.
"All the bones are gone."

"Maybe there's a dinosaur ghost hiding all the bones," Shaggy said.

"Roh no!" said Scooby.

"We have to help Uncle Ted find the missing bones," Velma said.

"He needs them for the exhibit," added Daphne.

"Let's look for clues, gang!" said Fred.

"Come on, Digger," said Uncle Ted to his dog. "You can help us look too."

Shaggy and Scooby looked
for clues.

They found a truck full of food.

"Like, it's a good thing we
found this truck," Shaggy said.

"Reah!" said Scooby.

But they did not find the
missing bones.

"Jinkies!" said Velma.

"Look at all these holes!

Somebody has been very busy

digging," she said.

The gang looked in each hole,

but they didn't find the bones.

All they found was one big rock.

"Let's make a fire," said Uncle
Ted. "We can look for the
missing bones in the morning."
Uncle Ted cooked hamburgers.
Then Scooby and Shaggy roasted
marshmallows.
"Like, I hope the dinosaur ghost
does not like marshmallows,"
Shaggy said.
"I wonder where Digger is?"
asked Uncle Ted. "Digger!
Oh Digger!"

Just then, Shaggy heard a noise.
"Let's go check it out," Velma
said.

"Rook!" said Scooby, pointing
in horror to the table.

"Oh no!" Daphne cried. "The
Scooby-Snacks are gone."

"Come on, gang," said Fred.
"We've got to find out who's
taking our things."

Scooby wanted to find the
Scooby-Snacks.

"Like, I bet the dinosaur ghost
took them," Shaggy said.

"Let's get to the bottom of this
mystery," Velma said.

"This way, gang!" said Fred.

The light from the full moon
helped Scooby see in the dark.
He used his nose to sniff for the
Scooby-Snacks and the bones.
It led him to Uncle Ted's dog.
Digger was bundled up in a
sleeping bag next to a mound
of dirt.
But there were no Scooby-Snacks
and no bones.
Then Scooby got a scent of
something…

Scooby used his super sense of smell and dug a hole in the dirt a few yards from Digger. Suddenly, Digger jumped up and began digging a big hole near Scooby and Shaggy.

"Good job, Scoob! Like, I think you found Digger's buried snacks," said Shaggy.

There in Digger's hole were the Scooby-Snacks and the dinosaur bones!

"Scooby, you saved the museum's dinosaur exhibit!" Uncle Ted said. "Now I just have to talk to Digger about what's okay to bury and what isn't."

"Scooby-Dooby-Doo!" barked Scooby.

The End

31901060304146